RAINY DAY KATE

by Lenore Blegvad
illustrations by Erik Blegvad

Margaret K. McElderry Books
NEW YORK

"Hello, hello.
Can Kate come to play?
Please can she come
and stay all day?

When can she come?
Can she come *today*?

She can?   She can!
Hip-hip hooray!"

When Kate comes

we will play hide-and-seek,

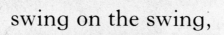

swing on the swing,

throw rocks in the creek.

When Kate comes

we will feed my mouse,

wear funny hats,

build us a house.

"Hello, hello.
What did you say?
Kate can *not* come out
on such a wet day?"

So that is that.
What a big flop!
It rains and rains.
Stop, rain, stop!
I am all alone.
Alone with *me*.
Nothing to do.
No one to see.

But I want fun!
So I have a plan.
I will *make* a Kate.
I know I can!

I need some pillows,
and some paper, too.

I need some string,
and paints and glue.

Here is her shirt.
Here is her hat.

Here is her face,

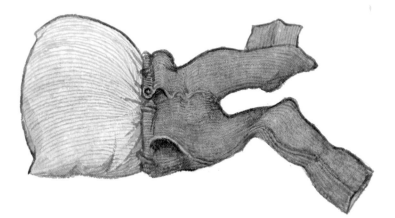

and her tummy *so* fat.

See my Kate?
How does she look?

Shall I tell her a story?
Shall I read her a book?

No, I know what!
This is what we can do!

Let's have a party!
All my toys can come too!

A party! A party!
With ice-cream and pie!

What fun we will have,
my friend Kate and I!

Originally published by William Collins Sons & Co., Ltd., London and Glasgow
Text copyright © 1987 by Lenore Blegvad
Illustrations copyright © 1987 by Erik Blegvad

Margaret K. McElderry Books
Macmillan Publishing Company
866 Third Avenue
New York, NY 10022

First United States Edition 1988

Printed and bound in Great Britain
by William Collins & Sons, Glasgow.

10 9 8 7 6 5 4 3 2 1

ISBN 0-689-50442-X

Library of Congress Cataloging-in-Publication Data is available.